KU-530-824

EDITH WHARTON

The Reckoning

PENGUIN BOOKS

PENGUIN CLASSICS

UK | USA | Canada | Ireland | Australia
India | New Zealand | South Africa

Penguin Books is part of the Penguin Random House group of companies
whose addresses can be found at global.penguinrandomhouse.com.

This selection published in Penguin Classics 2015
007

Set in 9.5/13 pt Baskerville 10 Pro
Typeset by Jouve (UK), Milton Keynes
Printed and bound in Great Britain by Clays Ltd, Elcograf S.p.A.

A CIP catalogue record for this book is available from the British Library

ISBN: 978-0-141-39756-6

www.greenpenguin.co.uk

MIX
Paper from
responsible sources
FSC® C018179

Penguin Random House is committed to a
sustainable future for our business, our readers
and our planet. This book is made from Forest
Stewardship Council® certified paper.

'If marriage was the slow life-long acquittal of a debt contracted in ignorance, then marriage was a crime against human nature.'

EDITH WHARTON
Born 1862, New York City, USA
Died 1937, Saint-Brice-sous-Forêt, France

'Mrs Manstey's View', Edith Wharton's first published story, appeared in 1891. 'The Reckoning' was published in 1902.

WHARTON IN PENGUIN CLASSICS
Ethan Frome
The Age of Innocence
The Custom of the Country
The House of Mirth
Three Novels of New York

Contents

Mrs Manstey's View

The view from Mrs Manstey's window was not a striking one, but to her at least it was full of interest and beauty. Mrs Manstey occupied the back room on the third floor of a New York boarding-house, in a street where the ash-barrels lingered late on the sidewalk and the gaps in the pavement would have staggered a Quintus Curtius. She was the widow of a clerk in a large wholesale house, and his death had left her alone, for her only daughter had married in California, and could not afford the long journey to New York to see her mother. Mrs Manstey, perhaps, might have joined her daughter in the West, but they had now been so many years apart that they had ceased to feel any need of each other's society, and their intercourse had long been limited to the exchange of a few perfunctory letters, written with indifference by the daughter, and with difficulty by Mrs Manstey, whose right hand was growing stiff with gout. Even had she felt a stronger desire for her daughter's companionship, Mrs Manstey's increasing infirmity, which caused her to dread the three flights of stairs between her room and the street, would have given her pause on the eve of under-taking so long a journey; and without perhaps formulating these reasons she had long since accepted as a matter of course her solitary life in New York.

She was, indeed, not quite lonely, for a few friends still toiled up now and then to her room; but their visits grew rare as the years went by. Mrs Manstey had never been a sociable woman, and during her husband's lifetime his companionship had been all-sufficient to her. For many years she had cherished a desire to live in the country, to have a hen-house and a garden; but this longing had faded with age, leaving only in the breast of the uncom-municative old woman a vague tenderness for plants and animals. It was, perhaps, this tenderness which made her cling so fervently to her view from her window, a view in which the most optimistic eye would at first have failed to discover anything admirable.

Mrs Manstey, from her coign of vantage (a slightly projecting bow-window where she nursed an ivy and a succession of unwholesome-looking bulbs), looked out first upon the yard of her own dwelling, of which, how-ever, she could get but a restricted glimpse. Still, her gaze took in the topmost boughs of the ailanthus below her window, and she knew how early each year the clump of dicentra strung its bending stalk with hearts of pink.

But of greater interest were the yards beyond. Being for the most part attached to boarding-houses they were in a state of chronic untidiness and fluttering, on certain days of the week, with miscellaneous garments and frayed table-cloths. In spite of this Mrs Manstey found much to admire in the long vista which she commanded. Some of the yards were, indeed, but stony wastes, with grass in the cracks of the pavement and no shade in spring save that afforded by the intermittent leafage of the clothes-lines. These yards Mrs Manstey disapproved of, but the others, the green ones, she loved. She had grown used to their disorder; the broken barrels, the empty bottles and paths unswept no longer annoyed her; hers was the happy faculty of dwelling on the pleasanter side of the prospect before her.

In the very next enclosure did not a magnolia open its hard white flowers against the watery blue of April? And was there not, a little way down the line, a fence foamed over every May by lilac waves of wistaria? Farther still, a horse-chestnut lifted its candelabra of buff and pink blossoms above broad fans of foliage; while in the opposite yard June was sweet with the breath of a neglected syringa, which persisted in growing in spite of the countless obstacles opposed to its welfare.

But if nature occupied the front rank in Mrs Manstey's view, there was much of a more personal character to interest her in the aspect of the houses and their inmates. She deeply disapproved of the mustard-colored curtains which had lately been hung in the doctor's window opposite; but she glowed with pleasure when the house farther down had its old bricks washed with a coat of

3

paint. The occupants of the houses did not often show themselves at the back windows, but the servants were always in sight. Noisy slatterns, Mrs Manstey pronounced the greater number; she knew their ways and hated them. But to the quiet cook in the newly painted house, whose mistress bullied her, and who secretly fed the stray cats at nightfall, Mrs Manstey's warmest sympathies were given. On one occasion her feelings were racked by the neglect of a house-maid, who for two days forgot to feed the parrot committed to her care. On the third day, Mrs Manstey, in spite of her gouty hand, had just penned a letter, beginning: 'Madam, it is now three days since your parrot has been fed,' when the forgetful maid appeared at the window with a cup of seed in her hand.

But in Mrs Manstey's more meditative moods it was the narrowing perspective of far-off yards which pleased her best. She loved, at twilight, when the distant brown-stone spire seemed melting in the fluid yellow of the west, to lose herself in vague memories of a trip to Europe, made years ago, and now reduced in her mind's eye to a pale phantasmagoria of indistinct steeples and dreamy skies. Perhaps at heart Mrs Manstey was an artist; at all events she was sensible of many changes of color unnoticed by the average eye, and dear to her as the green of early spring was the black lattice of branches against a cold sulphur sky at the close of a snowy day. She enjoyed, also, the sunny thaws of March, when patches of earth showed through the snow, like ink-spots spreading on a sheet of white blotting-paper; and, better still, the haze of boughs, leafless but swollen, which replaced the clear-cut tracery of winter. She even watched with a certain interest the trail of smoke from a far-off factory chimney, and missed a detail in the landscape when the factory was closed and the smoke disappeared.

Mrs Manstey, in the long hours which she spent at her window, was not idle. She read a little, and knitted numberless stockings; but the view surrounded and shaped her life as the sea does a lonely island. When her rare callers came it was difficult for her to detach herself from the contemplation of the opposite window-washing, or the scrutiny of certain green points in a neighboring flower-bed which might, or might not, turn into hyacinths, while she feigned an interest in her visitor's anecdotes about some unknown grandchild. Mrs Manstey's real friends were the denizens of the yards, the hyacinths, the magnolia, the green parrot, the maid who fed the cats, the doctor who studied late behind his mustard-colored curtains; and the confidant of her tenderer musings was the church-spire floating in the sunset.

One April day, as she sat in her usual place, with knitting cast aside and eyes fixed on the blue sky mottled with round clouds, a knock at the door announced the entrance of her landlady. Mrs Manstey did not care for her landlady, but she submitted to her visits with ladylike resignation. To-day, however, it seemed harder than usual to turn from the blue sky and the blossoming magnolia to Mrs Sampson's unsuggestive face, and Mrs Manstey was conscious of a distinct effort as she did so.

'The magnolia is out earlier than usual this year, Mrs Sampson,' she remarked, yielding to a rare impulse, for she seldom alluded to the absorbing interest of her life. In the first place it was a topic not likely to appeal to her visitors and, besides, she lacked the power of expression and could not have given utterance to her feelings had she wished to.

'The what, Mrs Manstey?' inquired the landlady, glancing about the room as if to find there the explanation of Mrs Manstey's statement.

'The magnolia in the next yard – in Mrs Black's yard,' Mrs Manstey repeated.

'Is it, indeed? I didn't know there was a magnolia there,' said Mrs Sampson, carelessly. Mrs Manstey looked at her; she did not know that there was a magnolia in the next yard!

'By the way,' Mrs Sampson continued, 'speaking of Mrs Black reminds me that the work on the extension is to begin next week.'

'The what?' it was Mrs Manstey's turn to ask.

'The extension,' said Mrs Sampson, nodding her head in the direction of the ignored magnolia. 'You knew, of course, that Mrs Black was going to build an extension to her house? Yes, ma'am. I hear it is to run right back to the end of the yard. How she can afford to build an extension in these hard times I don't see; but she always was crazy about building. She used to keep a boarding-house in Seventeenth Street, and she nearly ruined herself then by sticking out bow-windows and what not; I should have thought that would have cured her of building, but I guess it's a disease, like drink. Anyhow, the work is to begin on Monday.'

Mrs Manstey had grown pale. She always spoke slowly, so the landlady did not heed the long pause which followed. At last Mrs Manstey said: 'Do you know how high the extension will be?'

'That's the most absurd part of it. The extension is to be built right up to the roof of the main building; now, did you ever?'

Mrs Manstey paused again. 'Won't it be a great annoyance to you, Mrs Sampson?' she asked.

'I should say it would. But there's no help for it; if people have got a mind to build extensions there's no law to prevent 'em, that I'm aware of.' Mrs Manstey, knowing this, was silent. 'There is no help for it,' Mrs Sampson repeated, 'but if I *am* a church member, I wouldn't be so sorry if it ruined Eliza Black. Well, good-day, Mrs Manstey; I'm glad to find you so comfortable.'

So comfortable – so comfortable! Left to herself the old woman turned once more to the window. How lovely the view was that day! The blue sky with its round clouds shed a brightness over everything; the ailanthus had put on a tinge of yellow-green, the hyacinths were budding, the magnolia flowers looked more than ever like rosettes carved in alabaster. Soon the wistaria would bloom, then the horse-chestnut; but not for her. Between her eyes and them a barrier of brick and mortar would swiftly rise; presently even the spire would disappear, and all her radiant world be blotted out. Mrs Manstey sent away untouched the dinner-tray brought to her that evening. She lingered in the window until the windy sunset died in bat-colored dusk; then, going to bed, she lay sleepless all night.

Early the next day she was up and at the window. It was raining, but even through the slanting gray gauze the scene had its charm – and then the rain was so good for the trees. She had noticed the day before that the ailanthus was growing dusty.

'Of course I might move,' said Mrs Manstey aloud, and turning from the window she looked about her room. She might move, of course; so might she be flayed alive; but she was not likely to survive either operation. The room, though far less important to her happiness than the view, was as much a part of her existence. She had lived in it seventeen years. She knew every stain on the wall-paper, every rent in the carpet; the light fell in a certain way on her engravings, her books had grown shabby on their shelves, her bulbs and ivy were used to their window and knew which way to lean to the sun. 'We are all too old to move,' she said.

That afternoon it cleared. Wet and radiant the blue

reappeared through torn rags of cloud; the ailanthus spar-kled; the earth in the flower-borders looked rich and warm. It was Thursday, and on Monday the building of the extension was to begin.

On Sunday afternoon a card was brought to Mrs Black, as she was engaged in gathering up the fragments of the boarders' dinner in the basement. The card, black-edged, bore Mrs Manstey's name.

'One of Mrs Sampson's boarders; wants to move, I suppose. Well, I can give her a room next year in the extension. Dinah,' said Mrs Black, 'tell the lady I'll be upstairs in a minute.'

Mrs Black found Mrs Manstey standing in the long parlor garnished with statuettes and antimacassars; in that house she could not sit down.

Stooping hurriedly to open the register, which let out a cloud of dust, Mrs Black advanced to her visitor.

'I'm happy to meet you, Mrs Manstey; take a seat, please,' the landlady remarked in her prosperous voice, the voice of a woman who can afford to build extensions. There was no help for it; Mrs Manstey sat down.

'Is there anything I can do for you, ma'am?' Mrs Black continued. 'My house is full at present, but I am going to build an extension, and – '

'It is about the extension that I wish to speak,' said Mrs Manstey, suddenly. 'I am a poor woman, Mrs Black, and I have never been a happy one. I shall have to talk about myself first to – to make you understand.'

9

Mrs Black, astonished but imperturbable, bowed at this parenthesis.

'I never had what I wanted,' Mrs Manstey continued. 'It was always one disappointment after another. For years I wanted to live in the country. I dreamed and dreamed about it; but we never could manage it. There was no sunny window in our house, and so all my plants died. My daughter married years ago and went away – besides, she never cared for the same things. Then my husband died and I was left alone. That was seventeen years ago. I went to live at Mrs Sampson's, and I have been there ever since. I have grown a little infirm, as you see, and I don't get out often; only on fine days, if I am feeling very well. So you can understand my sitting a great deal in my window – the back window on the third floor – '

'Well, Mrs Manstey,' said Mrs Black, liberally, 'I could give you a back room, I dare say; one of the new rooms in the ex – '

'But I don't want to move; I can't move,' said Mrs Manstey, almost with a scream. 'And I came to tell you that if you build that extension I shall have no view from my window – no view! Do you understand?'

Mrs Black thought herself face to face with a lunatic, and she had always heard that lunatics must be humored.

'Dear me, dear me,' she remarked, pushing her chair back a little way, 'that is too bad, isn't it? Why, I never thought of that. To be sure, the extension *will* interfere with your view, Mrs Manstey.'

'You do understand?' Mrs Manstey gasped.

'Of course I do. And I'm real sorry about it, too. But there, don't you worry, Mrs Manstey. I guess we can fix that all right.'

Mrs Manstey rose from her seat, and Mrs Black slipped toward the door.

'What do you mean by fixing it? Do you mean that I can induce you to change your mind about the extension? Oh, Mrs Black, listen to me. I have two thousand dollars in the bank and I could manage, I know I could manage, to give you a thousand if – ' Mrs Manstey paused; the tears were rolling down her cheeks.

'There, there, Mrs Manstey, don't you worry,' repeated Mrs Black, soothingly. 'I am sure we can settle it. I am sorry that I can't stay and talk about it any longer, but this is such a busy time of day, with supper to get – '

Her hand was on the door-knob, but with sudden vigor Mrs Manstey seized her wrist.

'You are not giving me a definite answer. Do you mean to say that you accept my proposition?'

'Why, I'll think it over, Mrs Manstey, certainly I will. I wouldn't annoy you for the world – '

'But the work is to begin to-morrow, I am told,' Mrs Manstey persisted.

Mrs Black hesitated. 'It shan't begin, I promise you that; I'll send word to the builder this very night.' Mrs Manstey tightened her hold.

'You are not deceiving me, are you?' she said.

'No – no,' stammered Mrs Black. 'How can you think such a thing of me, Mrs Manstey?'

Slowly Mrs Manstey's clutch relaxed, and she passed through the open door. 'One thousand dollars,' she repeated, pausing in the hall; then she let herself out of the house and hobbled down the steps, supporting herself on the cast-iron railing.

'My goodness,' exclaimed Mrs Black, shutting and bolting the hall-door, 'I never knew the old woman was crazy! And she looks so quiet and ladylike, too.'

Mrs Manstey slept well that night, but early the next morning she was awakened by a sound of hammering. She got to her window with what haste she might and, looking out, saw that Mrs Black's yard was full of work-men. Some were carrying loads of brick from the kitchen to the yard, others beginning to demolish the old-fashioned wooden balcony which adorned each story of Mrs Black's house. Mrs Manstey saw that she had been deceived. At first she thought of confiding her trouble to Mrs Samp-son, but a settled discouragement soon took possession of her and she went back to bed, not caring to see what was going on.

Toward afternoon, however, feeling that she must know the worst, she rose and dressed herself. It was a laborious task, for her hands were stiffer than usual, and the hooks and buttons seemed to evade her.

When she seated herself in the window, she saw that the workmen had removed the upper part of the balcony, and that the bricks had multiplied since morning. One of the men, a coarse fellow with a bloated face, picked a magnolia blossom and, after smelling it, threw it to the ground; the next man, carrying a load of bricks, trod on the flower in passing.

'Look out, Jim,' called one of the men to another who was smoking a pipe, 'if you throw matches around near those barrels of paper you'll have the old tinder-box burning down before you know it.' And Mrs Manstey, leaning forward, perceived that there were several barrels of paper and rubbish under the wooden balcony.

At length the work ceased and twilight fell. The sunset was perfect and a roseate light, transfiguring the distant spire, lingered late in the west. When it grew dark Mrs Manstey drew down the shades and proceeded, in her usual methodical manner, to light her lamp. She always filled and lit it with her own hands, keeping a kettle of kerosene on a zinc-covered shelf in a closet. As the lamp-light filled the room it assumed its usual peaceful aspect. The books and pictures and plants seemed, like their mistress, to settle themselves down for another quiet evening, and Mrs Manstey, as was her wont, drew up her armchair to the table and began to knit.

That night she could not sleep. The weather had changed and a wild wind was abroad, blotting the stars with close-driven clouds. Mrs Manstey rose once or twice and looked out of the window; but of the view nothing was discernible save a tardy light or two in the opposite windows. These lights at last went out, and Mrs Manstey, who had watched for their extinction, began to dress herself. She was in evident haste, for she merely flung a thin dressing-gown over her night-dress and wrapped her head in a scarf; then she opened her closet and cautiously took out the kettle of kerosene. Having slipped a bundle of wooden matches into her pocket she proceeded, with increasing precautions, to unlock her door, and a few moments later she was feeling her way down the dark staircase, led by a glimmer of gas from the lower hall. At length she reached the bottom of the stairs and began the more difficult descent into the utter darkness of the basement. Here, however, she could move more freely, as there was less danger of being overheard; and without much delay she contrived to unlock the iron door leading into the yard. A gust of cold wind smote her as she stepped out and groped shiveringly under the clothes-lines.

That morning at three o'clock an alarm of fire brought the engines to Mrs Black's door, and also brought Mrs Sampson's startled boarders to their windows. The wooden balcony at the back of Mrs Black's house was ablaze, and among those who watched the progress of the flames was Mrs Manstey, leaning in her thin dressing-gown from the open window.

The fire, however, was soon put out, and the frightened occupants of the house, who had fled in scant attire, reassembled at dawn to find that little mischief had been done beyond the cracking of window panes and smoking of ceilings. In fact, the chief sufferer by the fire was Mrs Manstey, who was found in the morning gasping with pneumonia, a not unnatural result, as everyone remarked, of her having hung out of an open window at her age in a dressing-gown. It was easy to see that she was very ill, but no one had guessed how grave the doctor's verdict would be, and the faces gathered that evening about Mrs Sampson's table were awe-struck and disturbed. Not that any of the boarders knew Mrs Manstey well; she 'kept to herself,' as they said, and seemed to fancy herself too good for them; but then it is always disagreeable to have anyone dying in the house and, as one lady observed to another: 'It might just as well have been you or me, my dear.'

But it was only Mrs Manstey; and she was dying, as she had lived, lonely if not alone. The doctor had sent a trained nurse, and Mrs Sampson, with muffled step, came in from time to time; but both, to Mrs Manstey, seemed remote and unsubstantial as the figures in a dream. All day she said nothing; but when she was asked for her daughter's address she shook her head. At times the nurse noticed that she seemed to be listening attentively for some sound which did not come; then again she dozed.

The next morning at daylight she was very low. The nurse called Mrs Sampson and as the two bent over the old woman they saw her lips move.

'Lift me up – out of bed,' she whispered.

They raised her in their arms, and with her stiff hand she pointed to the window.

'Oh, the window – she wants to sit in the window. She used to sit there all day,' Mrs Sampson explained. 'It can do her no harm, I suppose?'

'Nothing matters now,' said the nurse.

They carried Mrs Manstey to the window and placed her in her chair. The dawn was abroad, a jubilant spring dawn; the spire had already caught a golden ray, though the magnolia and horse-chestnut still slumbered in shadow. In Mrs Black's yard all was quiet. The charred timbers of the balcony lay where they had fallen. It was evident that since the fire the builders had not returned to their work. The magnolia had unfolded a few more sculptural flowers; the view was undisturbed.

It was hard for Mrs Manstey to breathe; each moment it grew more difficult. She tried to make them open the window, but they would not understand. If she could have tasted the air, sweet with the penetrating ailanthus savor, it would have eased her; but the view at least was there – the spire was golden now, the heavens had warmed from pearl to blue, day was alight from east to west, even the magnolia had caught the sun.

Mrs Manstey's head fell back and smiling she died.

That day the building of the extension was resumed.

The Reckoning

'The marriage law of the new dispensation will be: *Thou shalt not be unfaithful – to thyself.*'

A discreet murmur of approval filled the studio, and through the haze of cigarette smoke Mrs Clement Westall, as her husband descended from his improvised platform, saw him merged in a congratulatory group of ladies. Westall's informal talks on 'The New Ethics' had drawn about him an eager following of the mentally unemployed – those who, as he had once phrased it, liked to have their brain-food cut up for them. The talks had begun by accident. Westall's ideas were known to be 'advanced,' but hitherto their advance had not been in the direction of publicity. He had been, in his wife's opinion, almost pusillanimously careful not to let his personal views endanger his professional standing. Of late, however, he had shown a puzzling tendency to dogmatize, to throw down the gauntlet, to flaunt his private code in the face of society; and the relation of the sexes being a topic always sure of an audience, a few admiring friends had persuaded him to give his after-dinner opinions a larger circulation by summing them up in a series of talks at the Van Sideren studio.

The Herbert Van Siderens were a couple who subsisted, socially, on the fact that they had a studio. Van Sideren's pictures were chiefly valuable as accessories to the *mise en scène* which differentiated his wife's 'afternoons' from the blighting functions held in long New York drawing-rooms, and permitted her to offer their friends whiskey-and-soda instead of tea. Mrs Van Sideren, for her part, was skilled in making the most of the kind of atmosphere which a lay-figure and an easel create; and if at times she found the illusion hard to maintain, and lost courage to the extent of almost wishing that Herbert could paint, she promptly overcame such moments of weakness by calling in some fresh talent, some extraneous re-enforcement of the 'artistic' impression. It was in quest of such aid that she had seized on Westall, coaxing him, somewhat to his wife's surprise, into a flattered participation in her fraud. It was vaguely felt, in the Van Sideren circle, that all the audacities were artistic, and that a teacher who pronounced marriage immoral was somehow as distinguished as a painter who depicted purple grass and a green sky. The Van Sideren set were tired of the conventional color-scheme in art and conduct.

Julia Westall had long had her own views on the immorality of marriage; she might indeed have claimed her husband as a disciple. In the early days of their union she had secretly resented his disinclination to proclaim

himself a follower of the new creed; had been inclined to
tax him with moral cowardice, with a failure to live up to
the convictions for which their marriage was supposed
to stand. That was in the first burst of propagandism,
when, womanlike, she wanted to turn her disobedience
into a law. Now she felt differently. She could hardly
account for the change, yet being a woman who never
allowed her impulses to remain unaccounted for, she tried
to do so by saying that she did not care to have the art-
icles of her faith misinterpreted by the vulgar. In this
connection, she was beginning to think that almost every
one was vulgar; certainly there were few to whom she
would have cared to entrust the defense of so esoteric a
doctrine. And it was precisely at this point that Westall,
discarding his unspoken principles, had chosen to des-
cend from the heights of privacy, and stand hawking his
convictions at the street-corner!

It was Una Van Sideren who, on this occasion, unconsciously focused upon herself Mrs Westall's wandering
resentment. In the first place, the girl had no business to
be there. It was 'horrid' – Mrs Westall found herself slipping back into the old feminine vocabulary – simply
'horrid' to think of a young girl's being allowed to listen
to such talk. The fact that Una smoked cigarettes
and sipped an occasional cocktail did not in the least
tarnish a certain radiant innocency which made her
appear the victim, rather than the accomplice, of her
parents' vulgarities. Julia Westall felt in a hot helpless

way that something ought to be done – that some one ought to speak to the girl's mother. And just then Una glided up.

'Oh, Mrs Westall, how beautiful it was!' Una fixed her with large limpid eyes. 'You believe it all, I suppose?' she asked with seraphic gravity.

'All – what, my dear child?'

The girl shone on her. 'About the higher life – the freer expansion of the individual – the law of fidelity to one's self,' she glibly recited.

Mrs Westall, to her own wonder, blushed a deep and burning blush.

'My dear Una,' she said, 'you don't in the least understand what it's all about!'

Miss Van Sideren stared, with a slowly answering blush. 'Don't *you*, then?' she murmured.

Mrs Westall laughed. 'Not always – or altogether! But I should like some tea, please.'

Una led her to the corner where innocent beverages were dispensed. As Julia received her cup she scrutinized the girl more carefully. It was not such a girlish face, after all – definite lines were forming under the rosy haze of youth. She reflected that Una must be six-and-twenty, and wondered why she had not married. A nice stock of ideas she would have as her dower! If *they* were to be a part of the modern girl's trousseau –

Mrs Westall caught herself up with a start. It was as though some one else had been speaking – a stranger who had borrowed her own voice: she felt herself the dupe of some fantastic mental ventriloquism. Concluding suddenly that the room was stifling and Una's tea too sweet, she set down her cup and looked about for Westall: to meet his eyes had long been her refuge from every uncertainty. She met them now, but only, as she felt, in transit; they included her parenthetically in a larger flight. She followed the flight, and it carried her to a corner to which Una had withdrawn – one of the palmy nooks to which Mrs Van Sideren attributed the success of her Saturdays. Westall, a moment later, had overtaken his look, and found a place at the girl's side. She bent forward, speaking eagerly; he leaned back, listening, with the depreciatory smile which acted as a filter to flattery, enabling him to swallow the strongest doses without apparent grossness of appetite. Julia winced at her own definition of the smile.

On the way home, in the deserted winter dusk, Westall surprised his wife by a sudden boyish pressure of her arm. 'Did I open their eyes a bit? Did I tell them what you wanted me to?' he asked gaily.

Almost unconsciously, she let her arm slip from his. 'What *I* wanted – ?'

'Why, haven't you – all this time?' She caught the honest wonder of his tone. 'I somehow fancied you'd rather blamed me for not talking more openly – before – . You almost made me feel, at times, that I was sacrificing principles to expediency.'

She paused a moment over her reply; then she asked quietly: 'What made you decide not to – any longer?'

She felt again the vibration of a faint surprise. 'Why – the wish to please you!' he answered, almost too simply.

'I wish you would not go on, then,' she said abruptly.

He stopped in his quick walk, and she felt his stare through the darkness.

'Not go on – ?'

'Call a hansom, please. I'm tired,' broke from her with a sudden rush of physical weariness.

Instantly his solicitude enveloped her. The room had been infernally hot – and then that confounded cigarette smoke – he had noticed once or twice that she looked pale – she mustn't come to another Saturday. She felt herself yielding, as she always did, to the warm influence of his concern for her, the feminine in her leaning on the man in him with a conscious intensity of abandonment.

He put her in the hansom, and her hand stole into his in the darkness. A tear or two rose, and she let them fall. It was so delicious to cry over imaginary troubles!

That evening, after dinner, he surprised her by reverting to the subject of his talk. He combined a man's dislike of uncomfortable questions with an almost feminine skill in eluding them; and she knew that if he returned to the subject he must have some special reason for doing so.

'You seem not to have cared for what I said this afternoon. Did I put the case badly?'

'No – you put it very well.'

'Then what did you mean by saying that you would rather not have me go on with it?'

She glanced at him nervously, her ignorance of his intention deepening her sense of helplessness.

'I don't think I care to hear such things discussed in public.'

'I don't understand you,' he exclaimed. Again the feeling that his surprise was genuine gave an air of obliquity to her own attitude. She was not sure that she understood herself.

'Won't you explain?' he said with a tinge of impatience.

Her eyes wandered about the familiar drawing-room which had been the scene of so many of their evening confidences. The shaded lamps, the quiet-colored walls hung with mezzotints, the pale spring flowers scattered here and there in Venice glasses and bowls of old Sèvres, recalled, she hardly knew why, the apartment in which the evenings of her first marriage had been passed – a wilderness of rosewood and upholstery, with a picture of a Roman peasant above the mantelpiece, and a Greek slave in 'statuary marble' between the folding-doors of the back drawing-room. It was a room with which she had never been able to establish any closer relation than that between a traveler and a railway station; and now, as she looked about at the surroundings which stood for her deepest affinities – the room for which she had left that other room – she was startled by the same sense of

23

strangeness and unfamiliarity. The prints, the flowers, the subdued tones of the old porcelains, seemed to typify a superficial refinement which had no relation to the deeper significances of life.

Suddenly she heard her husband repeating his question.

'I don't know that I can explain,' she faltered.

He drew his armchair forward so that he faced her across the hearth. The light of a reading-lamp fell on his finely drawn face, which had a kind of surface-sensitiveness akin to the surface-refinement of its setting.

'Is it that you no longer believe in our ideas?' he asked.

'In our ideas – ?'

'The ideas I am trying to teach. The ideas you and I are supposed to stand for.' He paused a moment. 'The ideas on which our marriage was founded.'

The blood rushed to her face. He had his reasons, then – she was sure now that he had his reasons! In the ten years of their marriage, how often had either of them stopped to consider the ideas on which it was founded? How often does a man dig about the basement of his house to examine its foundation? The foundation is there, of course – the house rests on it – but one lives above-stairs and not in the cellar. It was she, indeed, who in the beginning had insisted on reviewing the situation now and then, on recapitulating the reasons which justified her course, on proclaiming, from time to time, her adherence to the religion of personal independence; but she had long ceased to feel the want of any such ideal standards, and had accepted her marriage as frankly and naturally as though it had been based on the primitive needs of the heart, and required no special sanction to explain or justify it.

'Of course I still believe in our ideas!' she exclaimed.

'Then I repeat that I don't understand. It was a part of your theory that the greatest possible publicity should be given to our view of marriage. Have you changed your mind in that respect?'

She hesitated. 'It depends on circumstances – on the public one is addressing. The set of people that the Van Siderens get about them don't care for the truth or false-ness of a doctrine. They are attracted simply by its novelty.'

'And yet it was in just such a set of people that you and I met, and learned the truth from each other.'

'That was different.'

'In what way?'

'I was not a young girl, to begin with. It is perfectly unfitting that young girls should be present at – at such times – should hear such things discussed – '

'I thought you considered it one of the deepest social wrongs that such things never *are* discussed before young girls; but that is beside the point, for I don't remember seeing any young girl in my audience to-day – '

'Except Una Van Sideren!'

He turned slightly and pushed back the lamp at his elbow.

'Oh, Miss Van Sideren – naturally – '

'Why naturally?'

'The daughter of the house – would you have had her sent out with her governess?'

'If I had a daughter I should not allow such things to go on in my house!'

Westall, stroking his mustache, leaned back with a faint smile. 'I fancy Miss Van Sideren is quite capable of taking care of herself.'

'No girl knows how to take care of herself – till it's too late.'

'And yet you would deliberately deny her the surest means of self-defense?'

'What do you call the surest means of self-defense?'

'Some preliminary knowledge of human nature in its relation to the marriage tie.'

She made an impatient gesture. 'How should you like to marry that kind of a girl?'

'Immensely – if she were my kind of girl in other respects.'

She took up the argument at another point.

'You are quite mistaken if you think such talk does not affect young girls. Una was in a state of the most absurd exaltation – ' She broke off, wondering why she had spoken.

Westall reopened a magazine which he had laid aside at the beginning of their discussion. 'What you tell me is immensely flattering to my oratorical talent – but I fear you overrate its effect. I can assure you that Miss Van Sideren doesn't have to have her thinking done for her. She's quite capable of doing it herself.'

'You seem very familiar with her mental processes!' flashed unguardedly from his wife.

He looked up quietly from the pages he was cutting.

'I should like to be,' he answered. 'She interests me.'

II

If there be a distinction in being misunderstood, it was one denied to Julia Westall when she left her first husband. Every one was ready to excuse and even to defend her. The world she adorned agreed that John Arment was 'impossible,' and hostesses gave a sigh of relief at the thought that it would no longer be necessary to ask him to dine.

There had been no scandal connected with the divorce: neither side had accused the other of the offense euphemistically described as 'statutory.' The Arments had indeed been obliged to transfer their allegiance to a State which recognized desertion as a cause for divorce, and construed the term so liberally that the seeds of desertion were shown to exist in every union. Even Mrs Arment's second marriage did not make traditional morality stir in its sleep. It was known that she had not met her second husband till after she had parted from the first, and she had, moreover, replaced a rich man by a poor one. Though Clement Westall was acknowledged to be a rising lawyer, it was generally felt that his fortunes would not rise as rapidly as his reputation. The Westalls would probably always have to live quietly and go out to dinner in cabs. Could there be better evidence of Mrs Arment's complete disinterestedness?

If the reasoning by which her friends justified her course was somewhat cruder and less complex than her own elucidation of the matter, both explanations led to the same conclusion: John Arment was impossible. The only difference was that, to his wife, his impossibility was something deeper than a social disqualification. She had once said, in ironical defense of her marriage, that it had at least preserved her from the necessity of sitting next to him at dinner; but she had not then realized at what cost the immunity was purchased. John Arment was impossible; but the sting of his impossibility lay in the fact that he made it impossible for those about him to be other than himself. By an unconscious process of elimination he had excluded from the world everything of which he did not feel a personal need: had become, as it were, a climate in which only his own requirements survived. This might seem to imply a deliberate selfishness; but there was nothing deliberate about Arment. He was as instinctive as an animal or a child. It was this childish element in his nature which sometimes for a moment unsettled his wife's estimate of him. Was it possible that he was simply undeveloped, that he had delayed, some-what longer than is usual, the laborious process of growing up? He had the kind of sporadic shrewdness which causes it to be said of a dull man that he is 'no fool'; and it was this quality that his wife found most try-ing. Even to the naturalist it is annoying to have his deductions disturbed by some unforeseen aberrancy of form or function; and how much more so to the wife whose estimate of herself is inevitably bound up with her judgment of her husband!

Arment's shrewdness did not, indeed, imply any latent intellectual power; it suggested, rather, potentialities of feeling, of suffering, perhaps, in a blind rudimentary way, on which Julia's sensibilities naturally declined to linger. She so fully understood her own reasons for leaving him that she disliked to think they were not as comprehensible to her husband. She was haunted, in her analytic moments, by the look of perplexity, too inarticulate for words, with which he had acquiesced in her explanations.

These moments were rare with her, however. Her mar-riage had been too concrete a misery to be surveyed philosophically. If she had been unhappy for complex reasons, the unhappiness was as real as though it had been uncomplicated. Soul is more bruisable than flesh, and Julia was wounded in every fiber of her spirit. Her husband's personality seemed to be closing gradually in on her, obscuring the sky and cutting off the air, till she felt herself shut up among the decaying bodies of her starved hopes. A sense of having been decoyed by some world-old conspiracy into this bondage of body and soul filled her with despair. If marriage was the slow life-long acquittal of a debt contracted in ignorance, then marriage was a crime against human nature. She, for one, would have no share in maintaining the pretense of which she had been a victim: the pretense that a man and a woman, forced into the narrowest of personal relations, must remain there till the end, though they may have outgrown the span of each other's natures as the mature tree outgrows the iron brace about the sapling.

It was in the first heat of her moral indignation that she had met Clement Westall. She had seen at once that he was 'interested,' and had fought off the discovery, dreading any influence that should draw her back into the bondage of conventional relations. To ward off the peril she had, with an almost crude precipitancy, revealed her opinions to him. To her surprise, she found that he shared them. She was attracted by the frankness of a suitor who, while pressing his suit, admitted that he did not believe in marriage. Her worst audacities did not seem to surprise him: he had thought out all that she had felt, and they had reached the same conclusion. People grew at varying rates, and the yoke that was an easy fit for the one might soon become galling to the other. That was what divorce was for: the readjustment of personal relations. As soon as their necessarily transitive nature was recognized they would gain in dignity as well as in harmony. There would

be no farther need of the ignoble concessions and con-
nivances, the perpetual sacrifice of personal delicacy and
moral pride, by means of which imperfect marriages were
now held together. Each partner to the contract would
be on his mettle, forced to live up to the highest standard
of self-development, on pain of losing the other's respect
and affection. The low nature could no longer drag the
higher down, but must struggle to rise, or remain alone
on its inferior level. The only necessary condition to a
harmonious marriage was a frank recognition of this
truth, and a solemn agreement between the contracting
parties to keep faith with themselves, and not to live
together for a moment after complete accord had ceased
to exist between them. The new adultery was unfaithful-
ness to self.

It was, as Westall had just reminded her, on this understanding that they had married. The ceremony was an
unimportant concession to social prejudice: now that the
door of divorce stood open, no marriage need be an
imprisonment, and the contract therefore no longer
involved any diminution of self-respect. The nature of
their attachment placed them so far beyond the reach of
such contingencies that it was easy to discuss them with
an open mind; and Julia's sense of security made her
dwell with a tender insistence on Westall's promise to
claim his release when he should cease to love her. The
exchange of these vows seemed to make them, in a sense,
champions of the new law, pioneers in the forbidden

realm of individual freedom: they felt that they had some-how achieved beatitude without martyrdom.

This, as Julia now reviewed the past, she perceived to have been her theoretical attitude toward marriage. It was unconsciously, insidiously, that her ten years of happiness with Westall had developed another conception of the tie; a reversion, rather, to the old instinct of passionate dependency and possessorship that now made her blood revolt at the mere hint of change. Change? Renewal? Was that what they had called it, in their foolish jargon? Destruction, extermination rather – this rending of a myriad fibers interwoven with another's being! Another? But he was not other! He and she were one, one in the mystic sense which alone gave marriage its significance. The new law was not for them, but for the disunited creatures forced into a mockery of union. The gospel she had felt called on to proclaim had no bearing on her own case . . . She sent for the doctor and told him she was sure she needed a nerve tonic.

She took the nerve tonic diligently, but it failed to act as a sedative to her fears. She did not know what she feared; but that made her anxiety the more pervasive. Her husband had not reverted to the subject of his Saturday talks. He was unusually kind and considerate, with a soft-ening of his quick manner, a touch of shyness in his consideration, that sickened her with new fears. She told herself that it was because she looked badly – because he knew about the doctor and the nerve tonic – that he showed this deference to her wishes, this eagerness to screen her from moral drafts; but the explanation simply cleared the way for fresh inferences.

The week passed slowly, vacantly, like a prolonged Sunday. On Saturday the morning post brought a note from Mrs Van Sideren. Would dear Julia ask Mr Westall to come half an hour earlier than usual, as there was to be some music after his 'talk'? Westall was just leaving for his office when his wife read the note. She opened the drawing-room door and called him back to deliver the message.

He glanced at the note and tossed it aside. 'What a bore! I shall have to cut my game of racquets. Well, I suppose it can't be helped. Will you write and say it's all right?'

Julia hesitated a moment, her hand stiffening on the chair-back against which she leaned.

'You mean to go on with these talks?' she asked.

'I – why not?' he returned; and this time it struck her that his surprise was not quite unfeigned. The perception helped her to find words.

'You said you had started them with the idea of pleasing me – '

'Well?'

'I told you last week that they didn't please me.'

'Last week? – Oh – ' He seemed to make an effort of memory. 'I thought you were nervous then; you sent for the doctor the next day.'

'It was not the doctor I needed; it was your assurance – '

'My assurance?'

Suddenly she felt the floor fail under her. She sank into the chair with a choking throat, her words, her reasons slipping away from her like straws down a whirling flood.

'Clement,' she cried, 'isn't it enough for you to know that I hate it?'

He turned to close the door behind them; then he walked toward her and sat down. 'What is it that you hate?' he asked gently.

She had made a desperate effort to rally her routed argument.

'I can't bear to have you speak as if – as if – our marriage – were like the other kind – the wrong kind. When I heard you there, the other afternoon, before all those inquisitive gossiping people, proclaiming that husbands and wives had a right to leave each other whenever they were tired – or had seen some one else – '

Westall sat motionless, his eyes fixed on a pattern of the carpet.

'You *have* ceased to take this view, then?' he said as she broke off. 'You no longer believe that husbands and wives *are* justified in separating – under such conditions?'

'Under such conditions?' she stammered. 'Yes – I still believe that – but how can we judge for others? What can we know of the circumstances – ?'

He interrupted her. 'I thought it was a fundamental article of our creed that the special circumstances produced by marriage were not to interfere with the full assertion of individual liberty.' He paused a moment. 'I thought that was your reason for leaving Arment.'

She flushed to the forehead. It was not like him to give a personal turn to the argument.

'It was my reason,' she said simply.

'Well, then – why do you refuse to recognize its validity now?'

'I don't – I don't – I only say that one can't judge for others.'

He made an impatient movement. 'This is mere hair-splitting. What you mean is that, the doctrine having served your purpose when you needed it, you now repudiate it.'

'Well,' she exclaimed, flushing again, 'what if I do? What does it matter to us?'

Westall rose from his chair. He was excessively pale, and stood before his wife with something of the formality of a stranger.

'It matters to me,' he said in a low voice, 'because I do *not* repudiate it.'

'Well – ?'

'And because I had intended to invoke it as – '

He paused and drew his breath deeply. She sat silent, almost deafened by her heart-beats.

' – as a complete justification of the course I am about to take.'

Julia remained motionless. 'What course is that?' she asked.

He cleared his throat. 'I mean to claim the fulfillment of your promise.'

For an instant the room wavered and darkened; then she recovered a torturing acuteness of vision. Every detail of her surroundings pressed upon her: the tick of the clock, the slant of sunlight on the wall, the hardness of the chair-arms that she grasped, were a separate wound to each sense.

'My promise – ' she faltered.

'Your part of our mutual agreement to set each other free if one or the other should wish to be released.'

She was silent again. He waited a moment, shifting his position nervously; then he said, with a touch of irritability: 'You acknowledge the agreement?'

The question went through her like a shock. She lifted her head to it proudly. 'I acknowledge the agreement,' she said.

'And – you don't mean to repudiate it?'

A log on the hearth fell forward, and mechanically he advanced and pushed it back.

'No,' she answered slowly, 'I don't mean to repudiate it.'

There was a pause. He remained near the hearth, his elbow resting on the mantelshelf. Close to his hand stood a little cup of jade that he had given her on one of their wedding anniversaries. She wondered vaguely if he noticed it.

'You intend to leave me, then?' she said at length.

His gesture seemed to deprecate the crudeness of the allusion.

'To marry some one else?'

Again his eye and hand protested. She rose and stood before him.

'Why should you be afraid to tell me? Is it Una Van Sideren?'

He was silent.

'I wish you good luck,' she said.

III

She looked up, finding herself alone. She did not remember when or how he had left the room, or how long afterward she had sat there. The fire still smoldered on the hearth, but the slant of sunlight had left the wall.

Her first conscious thought was that she had not broken her word, that she had fulfilled the very letter of their bargain. There had been no crying out, no vain appeal to the past, no attempt at temporizing or evasion. She had marched straight up to the guns.

Now that it was over, she sickened to find herself alive. She looked about her, trying to recover her hold on reality. Her identity seemed to be slipping from her, as it disappears in a physical swoon. 'This is my room – this is my house,' she heard herself saying. Her room?

Her house? She could almost hear the walls laugh back at her.

She stood up, weariness in every bone. The silence of the room frightened her. She remembered, now, having heard the front door close a long time ago: the sound suddenly re-echoed through her brain. Her husband must have left the house, then – her *husband?* She no longer knew in what terms to think: the simplest phrases had a poisoned edge. She sank back into her chair, overcome by a strange weakness. The clock struck ten – it was only ten o'clock! Suddenly she remembered that she had not ordered dinner . . . or were they dining out that evening? *Dinner – dining out –* the old meaningless phraseology pursued her! She must try to think of herself as she would think of some one else, a some one dissociated from all the familiar routine of the past, whose wants and habits must gradually be learned, as one might spy out the ways of a strange animal . . .

The clock struck another hour – eleven. She stood up again and walked to the door: she thought she would go upstairs to her room. *Her* room? Again the word derided her. She opened the door, crossed the narrow hall, and walked up the stairs. As she passed, she noticed Westall's sticks and umbrellas: a pair of his gloves lay on the hall table. The same stair-carpet mounted between the same walls; the same old French print, in its narrow black frame, faced her on the landing. This visual continuity was intolerable. Within, a gaping chasm; without, the same untroubled and familiar surface. She must get away from it before she could attempt to think. But, once in her room, she sat down on the lounge, a stupor creeping over her . . .

Gradually her vision cleared. A great deal had happened in the interval – a wild marching and countermarching of emotions, arguments, ideas – a fury of insurgent impulses that fell back spent upon themselves. She had tried, at first, to rally, to organize these chaotic forces. There must be help somewhere, if only she could master the inner tumult. Life could not be broken off short like this, for a whim, a fancy; the law itself would side with her, would defend her. The law? What claim had she upon it? She was the prisoner of her own choice: she had been her own legislator, and she was the predestined victim of the code she had devised. But this was grotesque, intolerable – a mad mistake, for which she could not be held accountable! The law she had despised was still there, might still be invoked . . . invoked, but to what end? Could she ask it to chain Westall to her side? *She* had been allowed to go free when she claimed her freedom – should she show less magnanimity than she had exacted? Magnanimity? The word lashed her with its irony – one does not strike an attitude when one is fighting for life! She would threaten, grovel, cajole . . . she would yield anything to keep her hold on happiness. Ah, but the difficulty lay deeper! The law could not help her – her own apostasy could not help her. She was the victim of the theories she renounced. It was as though some giant machine of her own making had caught her up in its wheels and was grinding her to atoms . . .

It was afternoon when she found herself out-of-doors. She walked with an aimless haste, fearing to meet familiar faces. The day was radiant, metallic: one of those searching American days so calculated to reveal the shortcomings of our street-cleaning and the excesses of our architecture. The streets looked bare and hideous; everything stared and glittered. She called a passing hansom, and gave Mrs Van Sideren's address. She did not know what had led up to the act; but she found herself suddenly resolved to speak, to cry out a warning. It was too late to save herself – but the girl might still be told. The hansom rattled up Fifth Avenue; she sat with her eyes fixed, avoiding recognition. At the Van Siderens' door she sprang out and rang the bell. Action had cleared her brain, and she felt calm and self-possessed. She knew now exactly what she meant to say.

The ladies were both out . . . the parlor-maid stood waiting for a card. Julia, with a vague murmur, turned away from the door and lingered a moment on the sidewalk. Then she remembered that she had not paid the cab-driver. She drew a dollar from her purse and handed it to him. He touched his hat and drove off, leaving her alone in the long empty street. She wandered away westward, toward strange thoroughfares, where she was not likely to meet acquaintances. The feeling of aimlessness had returned. Once she found herself in the afternoon torrent of Broadway, swept past tawdry shops and flaming theatrical posters, with a succession of meaningless faces gliding by in the opposite direction . . .

A feeling of faintness reminded her that she had not eaten since morning. She turned into a side-street of shabby houses, with rows of ash-barrels behind bent area-railings. In a basement window she saw the sign *Ladies' Restaurant*: a pie and a dish of doughnuts lay against the dusty pane like petrified food in an ethnological museum. She entered, and a young woman with a weak mouth and a brazen eye cleared a table for her near the window. The table was covered with a red and white cotton cloth and adorned with a bunch of celery in a thick tumbler and a salt-cellar full of grayish lumpy salt. Julia ordered tea, and sat a long time waiting for it. She was glad to be away from the noise and confusion of the streets. The low-ceilinged room was empty, and two or three waitresses with thin pert faces lounged in the background staring at her and whispering together. At last the tea was brought in a discolored metal teapot. Julia poured a cup and drank it hastily. It was black and bitter, but it flowed through her veins like an elixir. She was almost dizzy with exhilaration. Oh, how tired, how unutterably tired she had been!

She drank a second cup, blacker and bitterer, and now her mind was once more working clearly. She felt as vigorous, as decisive, as when she had stood on the Van

Siderens' door-step – but the wish to return there had subsided. She saw now the futility of such an attempt – the humiliation to which it might have exposed her . . . The pity of it was that she did not know what to do next. The short winter day was fading, and she realized that she could not remain much longer in the restaurant without attracting notice. She paid for her tea and went out into the street. The lamps were alight, and here and there a basement shop cast an oblong of gas-light across the fissured pavement. In the dusk there was something sinister about the aspect of the street, and she hastened back toward Fifth Avenue. She was not used to being out alone at that hour.

At the corner of Fifth Avenue she paused and stood watching the stream of carriages. At last a policeman caught sight of her and signed to her that he would take her across. She had not meant to cross the street, but she obeyed automatically, and presently found herself on the farther corner. There she paused again for a moment; but she fancied the policeman was watching her, and this sent her hastening down the nearest side-street . . . After that she walked a long time, vaguely . . . Night had fallen, and now and then, through the windows of a passing carriage, she caught the expanse of an evening waistcoat or the shimmer of an opera cloak . . .

Suddenly she found herself in a familiar street. She stood still a moment, breathing quickly. She had turned the corner without noticing whither it led; but now, a few yards ahead of her, she saw the house in which she had once lived – her first husband's house. The blinds were drawn, and only a faint translucence marked the windows and the transom above the door. As she stood there she heard a step behind her, and a man walked by in the direction of the house. He walked slowly, with a heavy middle-aged gait, his head sunk a little between the shoulders, the red crease of his neck visible above the fur collar of his overcoat. He crossed the street, went up the steps of the house, drew forth a latch-key, and let himself in . . .

There was no one else in sight. Julia leaned for a long time against the area-rail at the corner, her eyes fixed on the front of the house. The feeling of physical weariness had returned, but the strong tea still throbbed in her veins and lit her brain with an unnatural clearness. Presently she heard another step draw near, and moving quickly away, she too crossed the street and mounted the steps of the house. The impulse which had carried her there prolonged itself in a quick pressure of the electric bell – then she felt suddenly weak and tremulous, and grasped the balustrade for support. The door opened and a young footman with a fresh inexperienced face stood on the threshold. Julia knew in an instant that he would admit her.

'I saw Mr Arment going in just now,' she said. 'Will you ask him to see me for a moment?'

The footman hesitated. 'I think Mr Arment has gone up to dress for dinner, madam.'

Julia advanced into the hall. 'I am sure he will see me – I will not detain him long,' she said. She spoke quietly, authoritatively, in the tone which a good servant does not mistake. The footman had his hand on the drawing-room door.

'I will tell him, madam. What name, please?'

Julia trembled: she had not thought of that. 'Merely say a lady,' she returned carelessly.

The footman wavered and she fancied herself lost; but at that instant the door opened from within and John Arment stepped into the hall. He drew back sharply as he saw her, his florid face turning sallow with the shock; then the blood poured back to it, swelling the veins on his temples and reddening the lobes of his thick ears.

It was long since Julia had seen him, and she was startled at the change in his appearance. He had thickened, coarsened, settled down into the enclosing flesh. But she noted this insensibly: her one conscious thought was that, now she was face to face with him, she must not let him escape till he had heard her. Every pulse in her body throbbed with the urgency of her message.

She went up to him as he drew back. 'I must speak to you,' she said.

Arment hesitated, red and stammering. Julia glanced at the footman, and her look acted as a warning. The instinctive shrinking from a 'scene' predominated over every other impulse, and Arment said slowly: 'Will you come this way?'

He followed her into the drawing-room and closed the door. Julia, as she advanced, was vaguely aware that the room at least was unchanged: time had not mitigated its horrors. The contadina still lurched from the chimney-breast, and the Greek slave obstructed the threshold of the inner room. The place was alive with memories: they started out from every fold of the yellow satin curtains and glided between the angles of the rosewood furniture. But while some subordinate agency was carrying these impressions to her brain, her whole conscious effort was centered in the act of dominating Arment's will. The fear that he would refuse to hear her mounted like fever to her brain. She felt her purpose melt before it, words and arguments running into each other in the heat of her longing. For a moment her voice failed her, and she imagined herself thrust out before she could speak; but as she was struggling for a word Arment pushed a chair forward, and said quietly: 'You are not well.'

The sound of his voice steadied her. It was neither kind nor unkind – a voice that suspended judgment, rather, awaiting unforeseen developments. She supported herself against the back of the chair and drew a deep breath.

'Shall I send for something?' he continued, with a cold embarrassed politeness.

Julia raised an entreating hand. 'No – no – thank you. I am quite well.'

He paused midway toward the bell, and turned on her. 'Then may I ask – ?'

'Yes,' she interrupted him. 'I came here because I wanted to see you. There is something I must tell you.'

Arment continued to scrutinize her. 'I am surprised at that,' he said. 'I should have supposed that any communication you may wish to make could have been made through our lawyers.'

'Our lawyers!' She burst into a little laugh. 'I don't think they could help me – this time.'

Arment's face took on a barricaded look. 'If there is any question of help – of course – '

It struck her, whimsically, that she had seen that look when some shabby devil called with a subscription-book. Perhaps he thought she wanted him to put his name down for so much in sympathy – or even in money . . . The thought made her laugh again. She saw his look change slowly to perplexity. All his facial changes were slow, and she remembered, suddenly, how it had once diverted her to shift that lumbering scenery with a word. For the first time it struck her that she had been cruel. 'There *is* a question of help,' she said in a softer key; 'you can help me; but only by listening . . . I want to tell you something . . . '

Arment's resistance was not yielding. 'Would it not be easier to – write?' he suggested.

She shook her head. 'There is no time to write . . . and it won't take long.' She raised her head and their eyes met. 'My husband has left me,' she said.

'Westall – ?' he stammered, reddening again.

'Yes. This morning. Just as I left you. Because he was tired of me.'

The words, uttered scarcely above a whisper, seemed to dilate to the limit of the room. Arment looked toward the door; then his embarrassed glance returned to Julia.

'I am very sorry,' he said awkwardly.

'Thank you,' she murmured.

'But I don't see – '

'No – but you will – in a moment. Won't you listen to me? Please!' Instinctively she had shifted her position, putting herself between him and the door. 'It happened this morning,' she went on in short breathless phrases. 'I never suspected anything – I thought we were – perfectly happy . . . Suddenly he told me he was tired of me . . . there is a girl he likes better . . . He has gone to her . . . ' As she spoke, the lurking anguish rose upon her, possessing her once more to the exclusion of every other emotion. Her eyes ached, her throat swelled with it, and two painful tears ran down her face.

Arment's constraint was increasing visibly. 'This – this is very unfortunate,' he began. 'But I should say the law – '

'The law?' she echoed ironically. 'When he asks for his freedom?'

'You are not obliged to give it.'

'You were not obliged to give me mine – but you did.'

He made a protesting gesture.

'You saw that the law couldn't help you – didn't you?'

she went on. 'That is what I see now. The law represents material rights – it can't go beyond. If we don't recognize an inner law . . . the obligation that love creates . . . being loved as well as loving . . . there is nothing to prevent our spreading ruin unhindered . . . is there?' She raised her head plaintively, with the look of a bewildered child. 'That is what I see now . . . what I wanted to tell you. He leaves me because he's tired . . . but *I* was not tired; and I don't understand why he is. That's the dreadful part of it – the not understanding: I hadn't realized what it meant. But I've been thinking of it all day, and things have come back to me – things I hadn't noticed . . . when you and I . . . ' She moved closer to him, and fixed her eyes on his with the gaze which tries to reach beyond words. 'I see now that *you* didn't understand – did you?'

Their eyes met in a sudden shock of comprehension: a veil seemed to be lifted between them. Arment's lip trembled.

'No,' he said, 'I didn't understand.'

She gave a little cry, almost of triumph. 'I knew it! I knew it! You wondered – you tried to tell me – but no words came . . . You saw your life falling in ruins . . . the world slipping from you . . . and you couldn't speak or move!'

She sank down on the chair against which she had been leaning. 'Now I know – now I know,' she repeated.

'I am very sorry for you,' she heard Arment stammer.

She looked up quickly. 'That's not what I came for. I

don't want you to be sorry. I came to ask you to forgive me . . . for not understanding that *you* didn't understand . . . That's all I wanted to say.' She rose with a vague sense that the end had come, and put out a groping hand toward the door.

Arment stood motionless. She turned to him with a faint smile.

'You forgive me?'

'There is nothing to forgive – '

'Then you will shake hands for good-bye?' She felt his hand in hers: it was nerveless, reluctant.

'Good-bye,' she repeated. 'I understand now.'

She opened the door and passed out into the hall. As she did so, Arment took an impulsive step forward; but just then the footman, who was evidently alive to his obligations, advanced from the background to let her out. She heard Arment fall back. The footman threw open the door, and she found herself outside in the darkness.